RAGGEDY ANN
AND THE
WONDERFUL WITCH

OTHER YEARLING BOOKS YOU WILL ENJOY:

Raggedy Ann Stories, JOHNNY GRUELLE

Raggedy Andy Stories, JOHNNY GRUELLE

Raggedy Ann and Andy and the Camel with the Wrinkled Knees
JOHNNY GRUELLE

Winnie-the-Pooh, A. A. MILNE

When We Were Very Young, A. A. MILNE

Now We Are Six, A. A. MILNE

The House at Pooh Corner, A. A. MILNE

The Wind in the Willows, KENNETH GRAHAME

Thimble Summer, ELIZABETH ENRIGHT

The Secret Garden, FRANCES HODGSON BURNETT

YEARLING BOOKS are designed especially to entertain and enlighten young people. The finest available books for children have been selected under the direction of Charles F. Reasoner, Professor of Elementary Education, New York University.

For a complete listing of all Yearling titles,
write to Education Sales Department, Dell Publishing Co., Inc.,
1 Dag Hammarskjold Plaza, New York, N.Y. 10017.

WORTH GRUELLE

RAGGEDY ANN
AND THE
WONDERFUL WITCH

by
Johnny
Gruelle

A YEARLING BOOK

Published by
DELL PUBLISHING CO., INC.
1 Dag Hammarskjold Plaza
New York, New York 10017

Yearling ® TM 913705, Dell Publishing Co., Inc.

ISBN: 0-440-47391-8

Reprinted by arrangement with The Bobbs-Merrill Company, Inc.

Printed in the United States of America

Second Dell Printing—October 1977

CHAPTER 1

Raggedy Ann, Raggedy Andy and their friend Ned Gnome were sitting on the log above the giggly brook, their feet hanging down in the cool water. As they splashed their feet up and down, they talked about the many adventures the Raggedys had had.

"Oh, we have had adventures that you might not believe, Ned Gnome, if we were to tell them," Raggedy Ann said.

"Yes!" Raggedy Andy chimed in. "You see, very often some creature finds out that Raggedy Ann has a magical Wishing Pebble and he tries to take it away from her."

"Is it a real-for-sure Wishing Pebble?" little Ned Gnome asked. "I have always wanted to see one. Will you show it to me, Raggedy Ann?"

"It is sewed up inside my cotton-stuffed body."
Raggedy Ann laughed.

"You see, Raggedy Ann lost the magical Wishing Pebble a couple of times," Raggedy Andy explained. "So we thought it would be best to have it sewed up inside her cotton-stuffed body, right beside her candy heart."

"And Raggedy Andy has a magical Wishing Stick sewed up inside his cotton-stuffed body, too," Raggedy Ann told little Ned Gnome.

"It isn't so good as Raggedy Ann's Wishing Pebble, though," Raggedy Andy said.

"Oh yes it is," Raggedy Ann said. "Raggedy Andy has made some very nice wishes with his magical Wishing Stick. But he hardly ever makes wishes."

"I forget half the time that I have the magical Wishing Stick sewed up inside my cotton-stuffed body—" Raggedy Andy laughed—"and besides, Raggedy Ann knows how to make better wishes than I."

"Oh no I don't," Raggedy Ann said, "but it is very nice for Raggedy Andy to say so! What would you like us to wish for you, Little Ned Gnome?"

"Oh, I do not wish for a thing, Raggedy Ann, thank you! I just wanted to see the magical Wishing Pebble and the Magical Wishing Stick work their magic."

"You can't see the magic even a little speck." Raggedy Ann laughed. "We just wish and the wish comes true."

"Let's wish for a lot of lollypops," Raggedy

Andy said, and, suddenly, there were the lollypops.

"Ah ha!" a loud voice cried. "I have just been waiting to see if you really did have a magical Wishing Pebble or a Wishing Stick. Now that I know you do, I'll thank you to hand them over to me. Quick, before I take them away from you!" And there was a strange-looking little old woman no larger than Raggedy Ann, her hand stretched out ready to grab something.

Raggedy Andy was just about to tell the little old woman she could not have either of the magical Wishing Things, when little Ned Gnome caught hold of Raggedy Ann and Raggedy Andy and whisked them up through the air, high above the deep, deep woods. The little old woman screamed for them to come back, but they only laughed.

"We will go up and bounce upon the great pop-corn clouds," little Ned Gnome said as he flew higher and higher, carrying Raggedy Ann and Raggedy Andy.

My, how the little old woman howled as she saw the three friends going up into the clouds! "Why, oh why, did I forget my flying broom?" the little old woman asked herself. Of course, no one answered her, for the Raggedys and little Ned Gnome were so high up in the air that they looked like tiny birds and could not hear her.

"I shall run home and get my flying broom," the little old woman cried. "And I will bet that I can catch them mighty quick!" Picking up her skirts, she ran away through the deep, deep woods.

The Raggedys were very pleased to be flying up to the clouds, for they knew just how nice and bouncy the great, fleecy clouds were. They are even better to bounce upon than soft bedsprings!

Little Ned Gnome and the Raggedys, way up on the tiptop of the great yellow "popcorn"

clouds, could look far down to the great earth below.

"Now," said little Ned Gnome, "we will all run and take a great big jump down to the next cloud below." So Raggedy Ann and Raggedy Andy each caught hold of one of little Ned Gnome's hands and they took a long run.

When they came to the edge of the top cloud, they jumped. Down, down they went. The air catching in Raggedy Ann's skirts made her whirl over and over until she landed beside Raggedy Andy and little Ned Gnome on the bouncy, soft cloud below.

From this cloud the three friends bounced high in the air again; for, you know, the big clouds are soft as feathers, but bouncy as rubber.

They bounced over and over again until they landed on the lowest cloud. Then they made their way to the top cloud and started all over again!

If the Raggedys and little Ned Gnome had not been so high up in the air, all the creatures in the deep, deep woods could have heard their laughter and happy shouts.

Now, of course, the Raggedys and little Ned Gnome did not know that the queer little old woman was a Witch and that she had a flying broom. So after they had bounced from the topmost cloud more times than they could count, they were surprised to see the Witch come riding up on her flying broom. And before the Raggedys could jump again, the old Witch had caught each of them by their arms.

"I shall take you home, and I shall take the magical Wishing Things away from you!" the old Witch cried. "I have always wanted a Wishing Pebble and a Wishing Stick."

The old Witch meant just what she said, and the Raggedys and little Ned Gnome could see that she was not fooling with them.

"But," Raggedy Andy cried, "the Wishing Pebble is sewed up inside Raggedy Ann's soft, cottony insides, and it is not right for you to take them away from us."

"Ha, ha, ha!" the old Witch laughed. "What do I care if the things are sewed up inside you? I guess I can snip an opening with my scissors and get the Wishing Pebble and Wishing Stick out, can't I?"

"Of course you can do that," Raggedy Ann said, "but it is wrong for you to take things that do not belong to you."

"Ha, ha, ha!" the little old Witch laughed again. "You just hurry and climb up in front of me on my flying broom!" And she gave Raggedy

Ann and Raggedy Andy such a yank she ripped two stitches out of each of their right arms.

All this time, little Ned Gnome was wondering what he could do to rescue his friends from the little old Witch.

"Even if I catch them quickly and fly away with them," he thought, "the little old Witch will be able to catch up with us, for I cannot fly very fast." And little Ned could not think of anything he could do to save the Raggedys.

But Raggedy Andy was watching for a chance to do something, and when the little old Witch pulled hard on Raggedy Ann's arm, he pulled her other hand so hard that the little old Witch was yanked right off her flying broom! Then, before she could get to her feet, little Ned Gnome ran and pushed her right off the edge of the tiptop "popcorn" cloud.

As she fell the little old Witch turned over and over. And each time she turned over, she let out a shriek. You see, she did not know that the

clouds were nice and soft and bouncy and she thought she would get a hard bump.

"Now, while the little old Witch is falling down to the next cloud, let's hurry down into the deep, deep woods and hide!" little Ned Gnome cried.

Just before they started, Raggedy Ann pushed the Witch's flying broom over the edge. "Now, she can get home all right!" Raggedy Ann laughed. "But she won't catch us, for we will be hidden long before she stops bouncing."

So little Ned Gnome flew down to the deep, deep woods with the Raggedys, and, as soon as they touched the ground, they all gave a happy shout, for there, not over twenty feet from where they landed, was a mud puddle of chocolate ice cream. Of course, an ice-cream mud puddle is nothing like an ordinary mud puddle, except that it looks a good deal like one.

The difference, though, is that an ice-cream mud puddle is just as good to eat as one of Mother's nicest puddings, and the grass all around it is covered with white frost, just like the frost you see in the garden in the fall. If you ever see an ice-cream mud puddle, you will know it immediately.

Little Ned Gnome and the Raggedys were pleased to see one, for they knew just how nice and sweet a chocolate ice-cream mud puddle is.

They pulled large leaves from a near-by bush

and in two minutes were eating the lovely chocolate ice cream and they forgot all about the mean old Witch.

It would have saved the three friends a lot of trouble if Raggedy Ann had not thrown the Witch's flying broom down to her when Little Ned Gnome pushed her over the edge of the popcorn cloud, down to the bouncy cloud below. For now, when the little old Witch stopped bouncing from her fall to the cloud below, she found her flying broom right near her.

"Ha, ha, ha!" she chuckled to herself. "They threw my flying broom down to me, so now I can hop right on it and fly after them." All that the selfish little old Witch could think about was getting the Raggedys so she could take the magical Wishing Things away from them. "I know where they are!" she howled to herself. "They are hiding in the deep, deep woods and they do not know that my flying broom is a magic broom and will take me to them."

Suddenly the little old Witch flew right to the spot where the Raggedys were enjoying their chocolate ice cream. As she reached to catch Raggedy Andy's arm, she laughed. "You thought I couldn't find you, didn't you? This time you shall not escape!"

But the little old Witch couldn't fool Raggedy Andy again. Before she could grab him, he gave the little old Witch such a push, he tumbled her right over backward into the ice-cream mud puddle.

"Wow, it's cold!" the little old Witch screamed as she splashed about trying to get to her feet again. Little Ned Gnome cried, "Quick, I know where to hide!" And before the Witch even knew what was happening, the three friends were running away through the deep, deep woods.

CHAPTER 2

By the time the Witch finally crawled out of the ice-cream mud puddle, the Raggedys and little Ned Gnome were far away.

The little old Witch picked up her flying broom and hobbled away to her home to change into clean clothes because her dress was covered with chocolate ice cream. The harder she ran, the more her teeth chattered. When she reached her little tumbly house, she was so cold she made a fire in the fireplace. But even after the fire was blazing, she was still so cold that she had to make a cup of tea to warm her up a bit.

"I wish the sun would melt all the ice-cream mud puddles in the world!" the mean little old Witch cried as her teeth chattered.

Thank goodness, her wish did not come true, for ice-cream mud puddles are very nice, and everyone who finds one always enjoys eating the ice cream. The little old Witch was just bad-tempered.

After the mean little old Witch had had her tea and was warm, she took off her cold, wet dress and put on a dry one. Then she said to her black cat with the green eyes, "Now I am going to catch the Raggedys and take the Wishing Pebble and the Wishing Stick away from them, no matter where they may be hiding."

Well, the Raggedys were hiding on the chute-the-chutes, right in the center of the deep, deep woods. The chute-the-chutes was down below a big clump of great trees where little Ned Gnome thought the old Witch would never find them as she flew over on her flying broom. But, just as they were starting down the long chute-the-chutes, who should appear at the bottom but the mean little old Witch.

"Now I shall catch you!" she cried as she stood

right at the bottom of the chute, with her arms stretched out to catch them.

The Raggedys and little Ned Gnome had all started down the chute-the-chutes together this time, but the little old Witch did not know they would come with such a hard bump.

She thought, because the Raggedys were very light, she could catch them easily, but she was fooled soon enough. The three friends were coming down so fast that the little old Witch was knocked down, and she bumped over and over so hard she rolled clear across the grass to the giggling brook and right into the deep pool! Then, before she could scramble out, the Raggedys and little Ned Gnome sped away through the woods.

"Now I shall have to run home and change my clothes again," the little old Witch cried, "but just wait till I catch that little Ned Gnome and the Raggedys! I shall take their magical

Wishing Things away from them and throw the Raggedys into the brook, too!"

So, instead of hopping upon her flying broom and chasing after the Raggedys and little Ned Gnome, the old Witch had to go home as quickly as the flying broom would carry her.

The green-eyed black cat had to laugh when the little old Witch, dripping wet, came into the tumbly house. But the Witch was so angry she did not even notice the green-eyed black cat.

"Just wait till I catch those Raggedys!" the little old Witch sputtered as she hustled out of her wet clothes into dry ones. "When I catch them, I'll bring them right here and snip them open with my little pair of scissors. Then I'll take the magical Wishing Pebble out of Raggedy Ann's cotton-stuffed body and the magical Wishing Stick out of Raggedy Andy's cotton-stuffed body! And I'll put both rag dolls in a tin can and tie a great big stone to the tin can and throw it into the brook. I'll bet they'll be sorry they pushed me into the chocolate ice-cream mud puddle and into the cold brook. Just wait!"

Little Ned Gnome and the Raggedys did not know how angry the little old Witch really was. And what is more, they did not care. In fact, all the Raggedys wanted the mean little old Witch to do was to go away and leave them alone to enjoy themselves. It really wasn't their fault if the mean little old Witch got into trouble each time she tried to cause them trouble. But it was just as Raggedy Ann said: "Isn't it funny? When someone is trying to bother you, it always makes him ill-tempered if you try to do something to help yourself." For, of course, the little old Witch grew crosser the more she thought about the three little friends.

Now little Ned Gnome, although his home was in the great yellow meadow, knew many hiding places in the deep, deep woods. He took the Raggedys right to the musical swings. But just as directly the magic flying broom carried the little old Witch to where they were. Out of the bushes she ran with a rope in her hands. This time she was going to tie the Raggedys when she caught them.

Raggedy Andy had just given little Ned Gnome a great push in the musical swing, but the little old Witch, seeing Raggedy Ann standing to one side, did not notice this. As the Witch ran toward Raggedy Ann, little Ned Gnome on the musical swing came flying down behind her, "BLOP!" and the swing hit the mean little Witch. Head over heels she went flying into a clump of molasses-candy bushes!

By the time she had pulled herself out, all covered with sticky taffy, the Raggedys and little Ned Gnome were far away, running through the

deep, deep woods. And so once more the little old Witch had to fly home to change her clothes. And the Raggedys had escaped again!

"You would think that when a person has been pushed from the top of the popcorn clouds, and has been pushed into a chocolate ice-cream mud puddle, and has been rolled into the cold giggling brook, and bumped by the musical swing into a clump of sticky molasses-candy bushes, that this person would leave us alone and would let us have our fun in peace!" Raggedy Ann said.

"The only thing is—" Raggedy Andy laughed —"the more the mean little old Witch is bumped and pushed about, the more nasty she becomes."

"Oh, I am quite certain of that," little Ned Gnome replied, "and soon she will follow us again and be hopping-mad to find all the time she has been having trouble, we have been having lots of fun!"

"Of course, I am sorry that she gets into trouble each time," Raggedy Ann said. "But maybe she will learn soon that she brings all her trouble upon herself."

The mean old Witch, however, had not learned this and she did not intend to let the Raggedys escape. So, as soon as she had washed and combed all the sticky taffy out of her hair and changed her clothes again, she hopped upon her magic flying broom and took after them once more.

"I'll bet they will not escape from me this

time!" the mean old Witch screamed to herself.

While the little old Witch was combing her hair and changing her clothes, the Raggedys and little Ned Gnome were running through the deep, deep woods. Quite out of breath, they were looking for a brook where they might get a drink.

Raggedy Andy had just discovered a soda-water fountain shooting right up from the center of a stone, when along came the old Witch.

"Aha!" the Witch cried. "Now I can catch you easily, because there is no chocolate ice-cream mud puddle you can push me into!" And with that she did catch Raggedy Ann and Raggedy Andy and started to drag them away with her. Suddenly, there was a loud noise in the bushes, and, grunting and squealing, little Percy Pig raced out, right under the mean little Witch.

Percy Pig was so excited that he did not see where he was running, and the little old Witch was so surprised that she dropped the Raggedys and held tight to Percy.

Percy Pig, even more startled now, just kept on going through the woods, this time carrying the mean old Witch right on his back.

"Now we can enjoy the lovely soda-water fountain." Raggedy Andy laughed as he filled three silver cups with the ice-cold soda water and handed one to Raggedy Ann and one to little Ned Gnome.

"I wonder what made little Percy Pig get so excited," Raggedy Ann said.

"Maybe he put his nose in a bees' nest!" little Ned Gnome suggested.

"When we have finished drinking our soda water, let's walk over to the bushes and see what frightened Percy Pig," Raggedy Andy said.

But just as they finished drinking and were ready to run to the bushes, little Percy Pig came walking up to the Raggedys, and, to their great surprise, caught them by their arms.

"I have them!" he called back into the bushes,

and out ran the little old Witch, crying, "That time Percy Pig and I fooled you!"

"The nice little old Witch has promised that I shall have Raggedy Andy's Wishing Stick and she will take Raggedy Ann's magical Wishing Pebble," little Percy Pig said. "That's why I came back and caught you!"

Raggedy Andy was just about to wrestle with Percy Pig when there was a flutter of wings and Wallie and Winnie Woodpecker came swooping down from a tree where they had been watching. Wallie Woodpecker landed upon Percy Pig's hat and Winnie Woodpecker landed upon the mean Witch's bonnet. Ratatatat the two woodpeckers pecked upon Percy Pig's head and the mean Witch's head.

"Ow, oh, they are after me," squealed Percy Pig. He dropped the Raggedys and ran away.

"Ouch, my head, my new bonnet!" the little old Witch shrieked as she picked up her skirts and ran away, too.

"Thank you, oh thank you, Winnie and Wallie Woodpecker!" the Raggedys exclaimed. While they sat and rested, they and little Ned Gnome offered sodas to the kind Woodpeckers. Suddenly Raggedy Ann laughed. "We never did find out why Percy Pig was so excited!"

Wallie Woodpecker answered, "Little Percy Pig had a good reason for squealing."

"What was it?" asked Raggedy Andy.

"Do you know Grampy Groundhog?" Wallie Woodpecker asked. "Well, sir!" he went on when the Raggedys and little Ned Gnome nodded their heads, "Grampy Groundhog had just finished planting a nice garden in front of his house when along came Percy Pig and rooted it all up! Little

Percy Pig is always putting his nose into other people's affairs. When he had finished rooting up the garden, he started rooting right before Gramp's front door. But Grampy had been watching from behind his front door, and he became so angry he bit Percy Pig's nose hard. Little Percy Pig's eyes filled with tears and he started squealing and running as hard and fast as he could!"

Raggedy Ann laughed. "Well, anyway, if it had not been for that, the mean old Witch would have captured Raggedy Andy and me that time!"

"Let's walk over and help Grampy Groundhog replant his garden," Raggedy Ann suggested. As the Woodpeckers flew away to join their friends, the Raggedys and little Ned Gnome walked through the bushes toward Grampy Groundhog's home.

CHAPTER 3

As the Raggedys walked up to Grampy Ground-hog's house, they found him grumbling about the damage Percy Pig had done. "Percy Pig ate up every root I had planted, and now I shall have nothing growing this summer!"

"Can't you find any more roots to plant, Grampy Groundhog?" Raggedy Andy asked.

"I went all over the deep, deep woods and could not find any," Grampy Groundhog replied, "and I am getting so old I cannot search farther. It would take a long, long time, too long for me, to find more roots."

"I tell you what we could do, Raggedy Ann and Raggedy Andy," little Ned Gnome said to his friends. "Let's run through the deep, deep woods to the candy-covered cooky bushes and bring back so many candy-covered cookies Grampy Groundhog will not want for something to eat for a long, long time."

"Are candy-covered cookies as good to eat as vegetables and roots?" Grampy Groundhog wondered.

Raggedy Andy laughed. "Usually vegetables are better for a person, but these cookies are magical. So just wait and see!"

Grampy Groundhog said, "It is too far for me to walk, so I will be fixing my front door while you are going after the cookies."

So the Raggedys and little Ned Gnome started running through the woods, when suddenly Raggedy Ann laughed. "Dear me, here we are running as fast as we can, when we could have stayed at Grampy's front door and wished for the candy-covered cookies!"

"Then let's go back and wish for the cookies to come to us," little Ned Gnome said. "I'd like to see how your magical Wishing Pebble works."

But just as the Raggedys and little Ned Gnome reached Grampy Groundhog's front door, the mean little old Witch scampered out from the bushes. She almost caught Raggedy Ann and Raggedy Andy, but Grampy Groundhog picked up his long-handled broom and cracked the Witch on her back. The mean little old Witch, howling and screaming, ran through the woods.

Then Raggedy Ann wished for Grampy Groundhog to have a large box filled with the

lovely candy-covered cookies. When Grampy Groundhog tasted them, he said, "Yum, yum, I had no idea they tasted this good!" After a while, he had eaten so many that he became thirsty, and Raggedy Ann wished for a fine little soda-water spring right beside Grampy Groundhog's door. Grampy Groundhog had never tasted soda water before and thought it was very, very good. "It is ever so much better than just plain water," he said.

"Yes, at times it is," Raggedy Ann agreed,

"but when you are very, very thirsty, there is nothing so good as plain, cold water." And with this, Raggedy Ann wished for a spring of plain, cold water to bubble up on the other side of Grampy's front door.

"Raggedy Ann and Raggedy Andy and little Ned Gnome, how can I ever thank you enough?" Grampy Groundhog asked.

"The nicest way to thank us," Raggedy Ann replied, "is to share your good fortune with your friends and neighbors!"

"Of course, that is just what I intended doing," Grampy Groundhog said. "But I wanted to slip away quietly and invite everyone and have a surprise party for you, my dear friends."

"Well, it can't be a surprise party for us, Grampy Groundhog—" Raggedy Ann laughed —"for we know about it; but you can invite your friends and have a surprise party for them."

"There won't be any surprise party except the surprise party I shall give you!" the mean little old Witch cried just then as she hopped out of the bushes and grabbed the Raggedys. Holding them tightly, she started to run, but *ker-splash!* she ran right into the spot where the soda-water and plain-water fountains met. As her feet flew out from under her, her arms went out, and the Raggedys, with one pull, got free. While they dashed into Grampy Groundhog's house, they could hear the little old Witch crying, "Oh, ow,

I'm all wet and cold again!" as she ran through the woods to her house.

Then the Raggedys asked Wallie Woodpecker to fly through the woods and invite all their friends to Grampy Groundhog's nice cookie and soda-water party. And you may be sure everyone had a fine, happy time.

"That was a dandy party, Raggedy Ann and Raggedy Andy!" Grampy Groundhog said, after the last of the guests had gone home. "They ate every one of the candy-covered cookies, but they couldn't drink the magical soda-water fountain dry! I'm glad, for I like soda water very much."

Raggedy Andy whispered to Raggedy Ann, as Grampy Groundhog lighted his corncob pipe and leaned back to have a quiet smoke. Then Raggedy Ann said, "Raggedy Andy wishes to try his magical Wishing Stick to see if he can wish a lot of candy-covered cookie bushes growing in your front yard, Grampy Groundhog."

"Can Raggedy Andy makes wishes come true

as well as you, Raggedy Ann?" Grampy asked.

"Yes, indeed!" Raggedy Ann replied. "Raggedy Andy has the magical Wishing Stick sewed up inside his cotton-stuffed body."

"Maybe if Grampy Groundhog and little Ned Gnome close their eyes, the Wishing Stick will work better," Raggedy Andy suggested.

So Grampy Groundhog and Ned Gnome closed their eyes tightly while the Raggedys held their hands over their eyes, because, being shoe-button eyes, the Raggedys could not close them.

Raggedy Andy had just started his wish when he felt himself caught from behind, and at that moment Raggedy Ann felt herself caught, too. Taking their rag hands away from their eyes, they saw that Percy Pig and his sister Penelope had slipped up quietly from behind and were holding them tight.

"Now we will have the magical Wishing Things!" Percy and Penelope cried as they started to run with the Raggedys. By this time Grampy Groundhog and little Ned Gnome had opened their eyes, for they knew something was wrong. Quickly, little Ned Gnome flew after the pigs and caught them by their curly tails, and held them tight while Grampy Groundhog cut two switches from a willow tree.

Whack, whack, whack, whack! Grampy Groundhog cracked the two pigs with his switches. Percy and Penelope Pig had never been switched like that before and they squealed as they never had before! They dropped the Raggedys in a hurry and scampered away through the woods.

"Just wait, we will catch you another time," they called back to the Raggedys. "We'll get the magical Wishing Things from you yet!"

But the Raggedys could not be scared by Percy and Penelope Pig, and so they went about their business. Raggedy Andy made his wish without closing his eyes and, in an instant, all around Grampy Groundhog's front yard were many candy-covered cookie bushes with all kinds of cookies on every bush.

But before they could even admire the cookie bushes, there was a sound like a big wind, and out from the deep, deep woods rushed the old Witch.

"Quick!" Grampy Groundhog cried. "Into my house, all of you!" And with a push he sent the Raggedys and Ned Gnome flying into his house.

Then he slammed the door and put his back to it.

"You can't come into my house, you old Witch," Grampy Groundhog cried. "The door is locked, and I will not let you in."

"Ha, ha, ha! You think you can fool me! I know the door isn't locked," the little old Witch screeched. "I will get you away from that door and then I will get into your house." The mean little old Witch rushed toward Grampy Groundhog, as though she would pull him away.

As soon as she came close enough, however, Grampy Groundhog bit her right hand on her finger, the largest one, with his sharp teeth. "Wow, ouch, you've hurt me!" the mean little old Witch howled as she ran away.

Grampy Groundhog laughed as he opened the door and let the Raggedys and little Ned Gnome out again. "Now we can have as many sodas and cookies as we want, for the mean little old Witch will not return for a long time." So he served sodas and candy-covered cookies to the

Raggedys and little Ned Gnome, and in three minutes all of them had forgotten about the mean little old Witch as they enjoyed themselves.

"I wish you and Raggedy Andy would stay right here in my cozy little house," Grampy Groundhog said to Raggedy Ann and little Ned Gnome. But the two Raggedys had already had so many strange and wonderful adventures that it did not worry them to know that a mean person was still after them. They were sorry that anyone was mean enough to wish another person harm, but they were not frightened.

"Why," said Raggedy Ann, "the mean old Witch is as easy to escape from as some other mean people we have met!"

"Oh, she is, is she?" the mean little old Witch cried as she poked her head in Grampy Groundhog's front room where the friends were eating candy-covered cookies and drinking sodas.

Grampy Groundhog turned to Raggedy Ann and said, "See what I told you? The mean little

old Witch will get you if you don't stay here with me."

"Ha, ha ha!" the Witch laughed. "I will get them anyhow!" And with that she came walking right in and caught each of the Raggedys by an arm.

Grampy Groundhog ran to his kitchen and when he returned he held his long broom in his hand. *Whack, whack!* the broom went, and it raised two bumps on the Witch's head. "Ow, oh, stop," the mean little old Witch howled as she fled out the door. "I will wait until the Raggedys leave Grampy Groundhog's house, that's what!"

"See?" Grampy Groundhog laughed. "You had better stay right here with me!"

"Thank you, Grampy Groundhog," the Raggedys said, "but we wish to go on. Someday we will come back and visit you again." And catching hold of Ned Gnome's hands, the two Raggedys walked away through the deep, deep woods, filled with fairies and everything. And they hummed to themselves as they went.

"I do not believe the mean little old Witch will bother us again," Raggedy Ann said.

"I hope the mean little old Witch stays right at home where she belongs," little Ned Gnome replied.

But he had hardly said this before Raggedy Andy gave a squeal of delight and went scampering through the woods as fast as he could go.

"Maybe Raggedy Andy saw the mean little old Witch," little Ned Gnome said.

But Raggedy Andy had seen something far nicer than a mean little old Witch. And, when Raggedy Ann and little Ned Gnome came to the place where Raggedy Andy had stopped, they soon knew why he had squealed so excitedly.

Raggedy Andy had discovered a large patch of pie plants!

Each plant had a lovely pie growing on it, and nearly all the pies were ripe and ready to eat.

Little Ned Gnome found a great big knife near a large pie and with this he cut out a big slice.

"Look out!" Raggedy Ann cried.

Little Ned Gnome did not have time to look

out, for he had no more than lifted out the big slice of pie when three blackbirds flew out.

The first blackbird snipped off little Ned Gnome's nose just as clean as could be.

The second tried to snip off Raggedy Ann's nose and the third blackbird tried to snip off Raggedy Andy's nose. But, of course, the Raggedys' noses were just painted on.

The three blackbirds flew to a high tree and, just as they settled there, the mean little old Witch put her head out of the bushes and laughed, "Ha, ha, ha! Those were magic pies that I planted, and I hid the trained blackbirds in that pie just to get your noses. Now if you want little Ned Gnome's nose, you will have to come to my house for it."

"We won't go!" little Ned Gnome said. "It doesn't hurt me a bit to lose my nose."

But the Raggedys felt sorry for little Ned Gnome and, even though his nose was only a very small one and red as a strawberry, they knew little Ned Gnome would miss it very much.

So, when the mean little old Witch whistled to the blackbirds and had put little Ned Gnome's nose in her pocket, the Raggedys and little Ned Gnome followed the Witch toward her home.

"There must be some way to get little Ned Gnome's nose away from the Witch," Raggedy Ann said. "We must try to think of how to do it as we follow her."

But, although Raggedy Ann, who was a very good thinker, thought and thought until she ripped two stitches out of the top of her head, she could not think of a way to get Ned Gnome's nose.

"I don't much care," little Ned Gnome said when they had almost reached the Witch's house. "Maybe I can find another nose better than that one. It was red as fire anyway, and I do not wish for you two to be captured by the little old Witch!"

Of course, the Raggedys did not wish to lose the magical Wishing Things either, but they wanted to get little Ned Gnome's nose back for him.

Finally Raggedy Andy thought of a plan. Raggedy Andy wished that little Ned Gnome's nose would get as hot as Geewhillikins!

Raggedy Andy did not tell the others what he had wished, but presently he saw the mean little old Witch begin to fidget, then to wiggle and twist, and finally give a jump in the air. "Ooo," she cried, "something is burning me!"

She tore off her apron, threw it on the ground and ran as hard as she could. "I can't carry a red-hot coal, even if it is little Ned Gnome's nose," she cried.

Raggedy Andy ran and picked up the apron and doused it up and down in the near-by brook. Then when the water had cooled little Ned

Gnome's nose, Raggedy Andy took it from the wet apron pocket and stuck it on little Ned Gnome's face again. Then the two Raggedys caught hold of Ned Gnome's hands and ran away from the Witch's house as fast as they could go.

"It was lucky you thought of such a good scheme, Raggedy Andy." Raggedy Ann laughed. "Now we had better hurry to a soda-water spring and get little Ned Gnome some soda after all that excitement."

CHAPTER 4

The Raggedys and little Ned Gnome had gone only a short distance before they heard someone cry, "Wait a minute!" and there behind them was the mean little old Witch again. In her hand she carried a pair of long-handled tongs.

"Where is it?" she demanded as she ran up to the three friends.

"Where is what?" Raggedy Ann asked in reply.

"Where is little Ned Gnome's nose, of course?"

"We shan't tell you," Raggedy Ann said.

"Ha! You are trying to hide little Ned Gnome's nose—that's what! But I see it now, right on his face, and I shall pinch it off again with my long-handled tongs!"

"Indeed, you will not!" little Ned Gnome said, starting to run.

"Ha, ha, I can run faster than you can!" the mean little old Witch replied as she took off after little Ned Gnome.

The mean little old Witch could run faster than little Ned Gnome, but little Ned Gnome was very clever. When he came to the patch of pies, he darted this way and that around the pies.

Just when the mean little old Witch had almost caught little Ned Gnome, she slipped, *ooo-ff!* Right into a ripe custard pie she went, and her feet slipped under her. Down she went, the long-handled tongs flying in the air!

Little Ned Gnome quickly picked up the tongs and, before the mean little old Witch could get to her feet he had given her long nose a hard pinch. With a howl, the little old Witch scampered away.

"Now you know how it would have hurt me if you had pinched my nose." Little Ned Gnome laughed. "I guess I will just keep the little old Witch's tongs. Then if she comes after us again, I can pinch her nose once more."

So on the three friends went through the deep, deep woods. As they came to a very thick part, little Ned Gnome said, "I smell something good!" He wiggled his little red nose. "The smell comes from right over there."

The Raggedys and little Ned Gnome walked in the direction of the good smell which made them hungrier than they had been, and in a short time they came to a bunch of queer-looking bushes.

"What strange flowers!" Raggedy Andy said when they were close to the bushes. "What do you suppose they can be?"

Some of the bushes had long reddish brown things on them and looked a great deal like the cattails you see growing along marshy places. Other bushes near by had long blossoms of a light-tan color.

But when the Raggedys and little Ned Gnome came up very close to the bushes, they found that they were hot dog and bun bushes.

"That's what I smelled!" Little Ned Gnome laughed as he reached up and picked one of the hot dogs.

Little Ned Gnome dropped the hot dog faster than he had picked it up and put his finger in his mouth. "Too hot!" he cried. "As hot as if it had just come out of the stove!"

"We will pick a bun first and then pick the hot dogs with the little old Witch's long-handled tongs!" Raggedy Ann said.

After they each had had a delicious hot dog on a bun, they looked about and suddenly Raggedy Ann cried, "Here's a pink lemonade spring!"

Now that they had finished eating, the three friends were ready to take a nap, but from the deep, deep woods came the voice of the mean little old Witch. As she rushed toward them, she cried,

"Aha! Now I have you and I shall pick off little Ned Gnome's nose again and he won't be able to pinch my nose because I have it tied up in a hanky!"

This was quite true, as the Raggedys and little Ned Gnome could plainly see. Raggedy Andy, quick as a flash, picked up the long-handled tongs and with them he pulled two hot dogs from the hot-dog bush. "Here," he said as he handed one to the Witch.

The mean little old Witch could not see very well and did not know that Raggedy Andy was handing her a boiling-hot hot dog. But as soon as she caught hold of the hot dog, she let out a loud squeal and jumped right smack dab into the hot-dog bush. The hot dogs hit against her and burned her at each step.

"*Wow, ooh, oh, ow!*" the mean little old Witch howled. "They must be hornets!"

The Raggedys knew they could not fool the mean little old Witch again with the hot dogs, so, catching hold of little Ned Gnome's hands, they went running through the woods with the little mean old Witch following right behind them.

Little Ned Gnome was getting pretty tired when Raggedy Ann saw a queer little square opening in the ground. "Quick!" she cried. "Let's crawl through this little square tunnel." She let go of little Ned Gnome's hand and, followed by her friends, she crawled as fast as her cotton-

stuffed legs would carry her right down through
the dark square tunnel. When she reached the
other end of the long square tunnel, she turned
to help little Ned Gnome through. As she turned,
she saw a sign which read: "Pull this lever to
start the Paddling Machine."

When they were all safely out of the tunnel,
Raggedy Ann pulled the lever. They could hear
the sound of the paddles moving. Then they
heard the sound of the paddles whacking something and they knew it must be the little old
mean Witch, for they could hear her shrieking.

"Listen to that racket!" little Ned Gnome said
as he caught hold of the Raggedys by the hand
and all three started running away.

Now, when the old Witch finally came out of
the queer tunnel, she did not feel like chasing
the Raggedys any longer.

"I am going home to rest," she shouted. "But
just you wait, I'll catch you yet, and when I do,

look out! I shall take the Wishing Pebble and the Wishing Stick away from you, and then I shall wish for you to go through the Paddling Machine, too."

Although the Raggedys and little Ned Gnome had left the little old mean Witch far behind, they could hear her words echoing through the woods, but they were on their way back to the pink-lemonade spring and were not frightened by the Witch.

After they had their drink, they could well laugh at the adventures they had just had with the little old mean Witch.

"But we must not forget," said Raggedy Ann, "that the Witch promised us that when she caught us, she would take the Wishing Pebble and Wishing Stick away from us and make us go through the Paddling Machine."

"We must try not to let her catch you," little Ned Gnome said.

"Oh, it would not hurt Raggedy Ann nor me if we went through the Paddling Machine!" Raggedy Ann said. "But if you had to go through it, I guess it would hurt you as much as it did the old Witch."

"Then I wouldn't want to go through the Paddling Machine." Little Ned Gnome laughed.

"Aha! I heard you that time," the mean little old Witch howled just then, poking her head through the bushes. "So you wouldn't like to go through the Paddling Machine, little Ned Gnome?"

"No indeed," little Ned Gnome said. "And I shall start running away from you right now!"

"And we shall run right with you, little Ned Gnome," the Raggedys said. And the three friends started running, for they expected the mean little old Witch to run after them.

But, instead, the mean little old Witch sat down on the grass and took a bunch of strange things out of her pocket. As she drew a circle on the ground, she said, "I will put all these magical charms in the circle and hop around it and then we shall see!"

There, inside the circle, were the left hind legs of a bluebottle fly, two little red beads tied together with a blue string, a small shell, two bent pins, and a cork out of a catsup bottle.

As she hopped around all these magical charms with her left foot, the Witch wished for

WORTH GRUELLE

a dandy Paddling Machine to catch the Raggedys and little Ned Gnome.

The next thing the Raggedys and little Ned Gnome knew, they were in a long square chute with a lot of paddles in it. And the paddles were doing a dandy job of paddling. But Raggedy Andy was on one side of little Ned Gnome and Raggedy Ann was on the other side, so instead of the paddles hitting little Ned Gnome, they hit the soft cotton-stuffed bodies of the two rag dolls, and no one was hurt.

The little old mean Witch was at the other end of the chute, waiting to hear little Ned Gnome's squeals. But when the three friends came out of the machine laughing and giggling, the Witch was so angry that she turned right around to go home and hunt up more magical charms. And the Raggedys with little Ned Gnome went back to the pink-lemonade spring to get some more drinks.

CHAPTER 5

"Did you notice how angry the Witch was when she saw us laughing as we came out of the Paddling Machine?" little Ned Gnome asked as he handed Raggedy Ann and Raggedy Andy a pink lemonade.

"Indeed I did!" Raggedy Ann and Raggedy Andy both said.

"She said she was going home to hunt for more magical charms, so that she might work more magic on us!" little Ned Gnome said.

"Well," Raggedy Ann said, "each time the mean little old Witch tries to harm us, she always harms herself! Let's hope she grows tired pretty soon and let us alone so we may have fun."

"I think we have fun as it is!" Raggedy Ann said.

"So do I." Little Ned Gnome laughed. Suddenly his little red nose turned pale. He took off his cap and began hitting the air all around his head.

"What is the trouble with little Ned Gnome?" Raggedy Andy asked as little Ned Gnome went running away through the deep, deep woods, striking all about him with his little hat.

"I do not know," replied Raggedy Ann.

"Ha! ha! So you don't know, Miss Raggedy Ann!" The mean little old Witch laughed as she popped out of the bushes and caught Raggedy Ann by the arm. "Then I shall tell you. With all my magical charms I have made many invisible bumblebees to chase little Ned Gnome away from you so that I might catch you and Raggedy Andy."

"That was a very unkind thing to do, and you should be ashamed of yourself," Raggedy Ann said.

"Come here, Raggedy Ann!" the mean little old Witch cried as she tried to catch the Raggedys.

"Indeed I shan't!" Raggedy Andy shouted as he hopped out of the Witch's way. "I wish the invisible bumblebees would quit chasing little Ned Gnome and chase you!"

"Ha, ha, there is no fear of that, for the invisible bumblebees are magical and they were made through my own magic charms."

Then, seeing that she could not catch Raggedy Andy, the Witch said, "Well, anyway, I've caught Raggedy Ann, and she has the Wishing Pebble sewed up inside her cotton-stuffed body. So I shall take her home!"

But the Witch had dragged Raggedy Ann only a few feet when she started hopping about and howling, "Wow, they are after me!" She quickly dropped Raggedy Ann and started hitting about herself with her hat.

"Aha!" Raggedy Andy cried. "Your invisible bumblebees have come right after you as I wished. So now you know how little Ned Gnome felt when they chased him. You had better run home and undo your magic invisible bumblebees!"

And the mean old Witch did run for home as fast as she could.

"I never got stung once!" Little Ned Gnome laughed as he came up to the Raggedys. Together they watched the Witch disappear through the deep, deep woods, lickety split!

"Let's go and visit Grampy Groundhog," Raggedy Ann suggested. "Maybe he will invite us to have some candy-covered cookies."

So the three friends started off through the deep, deep woods to visit Grampy Groundhog, but they had not gone far when along came the little old Witch, sailing after them on her flying broom. At the end of her nose was a big white bandage and she was howling, "Look at what you did to me! It is all your fault that one of the invisible bumblebees stung my nose, and I had to put baking soda on it." As she flew around their heads, she went on, "But you shan't escape from me this time! I've made an invisible string to tie you with, and no matter how fast you run, the invisible string will catch up with you."

In just a few seconds the Raggedys and little Ned Gnome felt the invisible string tighten around their legs and they could not run a step, or even move for that matter.

"Aha!" The Witch laughed. "Now I have you!" And catching one end of the invisible string, she got on her flying broom and went sailing through the woods, dragging Raggedy Ann, Raggedy Andy and little Ned Gnome right behind her.

Of course, when the Witch dragged the Raggedys, it did not hurt them a bit as they bumped about over the stones and sticks. It did hurt little Ned Gnome and he cried as the stones scratched and hurt him. Raggedy Ann could not let her friend be hurt this way and, after a minute, she thought of a way to help little Ned Gnome. "I wish the mean little old Witch's broom would stop flying!" she thought to herself.

When the flying broom stopped suddenly, the old Witch continued to go through the air; over and over she rolled until she came to a stop, "*Blump*," smack dab against a large, fat tree trunk!

"Umph!" the mean little old witch cried, for it had almost knocked the breath out of her. "What happened to my flying broom? It never acted that way before."

Raggedy Ann did not answer the mean little old Witch, and, of course, Raggedy Andy and little Ned Gnome did not know that Raggedy Ann had wished the flying broom to come to such a sudden stop.

The mean little old Witch finally got to her feet and pulled on her flying broom, but still it

would not budge. "Something must have happened to my flying broom!" she cried.

Raggedy Andy suggested, "Maybe someone has got into your house and is wrecking your magical charms!"

"I'll bet that is what has happened," the Witch said. "Anyway, you can't get away from my magical invisible string, so I will run home and see what is the matter." And away she went to her house in the woods.

Then Raggedy Ann wiggled her shoe-button eyes at little Ned Gnome and Raggedy Andy and, catching their hands, she started running with them.

"I made the Witch's flying broom stop!" Raggedy Ann said after they had run a long way. "And then I wished for the invisible string to stop pulling."

"Ha, ha!" Little Ned Gnome laughed. "Won't the Witch be surprised to find us gone when she comes back to her flying broom?"

Now, when the mean little old Witch returned to the woods where she had left the three friends and found that they had escaped again, she was very, very angry.

"Just you wait!" she said to no one in particular, for there was no one listening. "I'll bet the next time I catch them, they will not escape!" After she found her flying broom right where she had left it, she was able to pick it up and get on it. So, calling out, "Giddap, flying broom! Take me to wherever Raggedy Ann and Raggedy Andy are hiding," she flew through the woods, right to the soda-water spring, for that was where the Raggedys and little Ned Gnome were.

Raggedy Ann and Raggedy Andy and little Ned Gnome were busy drinking lovely vanilla sodas and eating candy-covered cookies.

The Witch did not know they were drinking magical soda water. She thought it was just plain everyday water. And she was so mean she wanted to spoil it for them. So she picked out of her apron pocket a magic charm, a piece of blue bottle glass, and she wished, "I wish the water would turn green!" as she rubbed the charm three times with her left hand.

And, of course, as soon as she had said this, the soda water did turn green.

"Dear me!" little Ned Gnome said. "What is the matter with our soda-water spring, Raggedy Ann?"

Raggedy Ann looked at the spring, then dipped a cup full and tasted it. She did not know that the Witch had changed the water, or indeed that the Witch was peeping out at them.

"Oh goodie!" Raggedy Ann said, when she tasted the new green soda. "It has changed from vanilla flavor to lime and is ever so much better than before." And she dipped cups for Raggedy Andy and little Ned Gnome.

When the mean little old Witch saw this, she stamped her feet and decided she must not let the Raggedys escape again. "I'll get Raggedy Ann's Wishing Pebble and Raggedy Andy's Wishing Stick next time!" she howled as she flew over their heads and into the woods. But the three friends were too busy laughing and having fun to pay attention to her.

CHAPTER 6

When the mean old Witch reached her home, she found to her surprise that she had a visitor waiting for her. The visitor, who looked enough like her to be her sister, was her cousin, Winda, who exclaimed, "Why, Wanda, whatever has happened to your nose?"

Tearing the bandage off her nose, the little old mean Witch, whose name was Wanda Witch, explained about the invisible bumblebees and the Raggedys and the Wishing Pebble and the Wishing Stick. When she finished, she asked Winda, "Will you help me capture the Raggedys and little Ned Gnome?"

Winda took a little bag of charms from her apron pocket. "Of course I will, and we will use all of my magic charms with yours, so that they shall not escape again!"

The two Witches got into the magical flying broom and sailed through the woods after the Raggedys and little Ned Gnome who had decided to visit some of their friends. When they heard the noise of the magical flying broom the three of them crawled into a hole in a tree as fast as they could.

But the flying broom brought the two Witches right to the tree and the Raggedys could hear the Witches exclaim, "Aha! Now we have them! They cannot get out of the hole in the tree and we will reach in and pull them out."

Inside the tree, Raggedy Ann could see that there were now two Witches instead of one and she said, "Oh dear, the mean little old Witch has got one of her Witch friends to help her! We will have to think hard to get out of this."

While the Raggedys were thinking so hard that they nearly burst the seams in their heads, Winda Witch wondered, "Maybe the Raggedys will bite if we stick our hands into the hole of the tree!"

"No, they can't," Wanda told her cousin, "for they are only rag dolls and have no teeth." And the two Witches reached into the hole in the tree to catch the Raggedys. But at that moment, the hole in the tree, thanks to the Raggedys' wishing, closed tight on their hands and held the Witches fast.

"Now we must run out the other side of the tree," Raggedy Ann said and, catching little Ned Gnome's right hand and Raggedy Andy's left hand, she ran and ran until she came to a clearing where a magical popcorn-ball tree was growing.

The branches of the tree held snowy white popcorn balls which dropped off and fell right into a candy spring below. When the popcorn balls had rolled in the candy spring and were covered with sweet, sticky candy, they shot up into the air and finally fell on the ground, waiting for someone to pick them up and eat them.

"It's a popcorn-ball ground!" Raggedy Andy laughed with surprise as he picked up one of the balls and tasted it.

"I wonder how long the two mean little old Witches will be fastened by their hands to the hole in the tree?" little Ned Gnome said as he munched on a popcorn ball.

"I do not know," Raggedy Ann replied as she picked up another popcorn ball.

And the two Witches, Winda and Wanda, were wondering the same thing.

"How will we ever get our hands out of this tree?" Wanda Witch asked. "Even though you have only one hand stuck, it is just as bad as if both hands were in there, like mine!"

"I do not know how I can help," Winda Witch

replied. "The Raggedys must have made the hole close upon our hands. With the magical Wishing Things, it was easy for them to catch us."

But Wanda Witch had been thinking and soon she cried out, "I know! If you can reach into my pocket with your free hand and get out my piece of blue bottle glass, I will charm the hole in the tree, and we will get our hands out."

So Winda Witch reached into Wanda's pocket and got out the piece of blue bottle glass which was a magic charm.

Then Wanda Witch held the charm in her left hand, for her right hand was fastened in the tree and said, "Higgledy-piggledy-my-black-hen!"

which is a very magical thing to say if you have a piece of blue bottle glass.

The hole in the tree opened and the two mean little old Witches were free.

"Now we will get upon the flying broom and soon catch the Raggedys," Wanda Witch cried.

When the flying broom came up to the Raggedys, there they were, with little Ned Gnome, eating popcorn balls under the popcorn-ball tree.

"Ha! ha! ha! you thought we would still be fastened in the tree, didn't you?" Wanda Witch howled at the Raggedys.

But before either of the two little old Witches could get off from the flying broom, Raggedy Andy made a wish to himself and before you could say, "Three little pigs went to market," the flying broom kicked up in the air just like a bucking horse. It rolled the two mean little old Witches right into the sticky candied popcorn balls. When the Witches managed to stand up, it looked as if they had been out in a hard snowstorm, for the candied popcorn was sticking all over their clothes and in their hair, and even on their long noses!

"Ugh!" Wanda and Winda Witch cried. "This is too sticky! Let's go home and wash the candied popcorn balls out of our hair and then we will come back and capture you!"

"Hurry up!" Raggedy Andy laughed. "For we may not be here if you stay away too long."

The two little old Witches did not reply to this, for they knew the flying broom would find the Raggedys wherever they might be hiding. As they flew away, Wanda Witch said to Winda, "It won't take us very long, and the Raggedys will not escape next time."

When the two mean little old Witches had cleaned all the candy and popcorn off their clothes and faces, they hopped upon the flying broom and cried, "Take us to where the Raggedys are hiding!" And the flying broom took them through the deep, deep woods.

Now it just happened that the Raggedys and little Ned Gnome had stopped at the giggling brook to get a cold drink, and when they heard the two Witches coming after them on the flying broom, little Ned Gnome said, "Raggedy Ann, why don't you wish for the flying broom to kick up again and throw the Witches into the water? Then they will have to go home again to change their clothes."

But Raggedy Ann said, "I will make a wish when the two little Witches get close, and it will surprise them I bet!"

Through the trees came the flying broom and the two Witches jumped off right beside the Raggedys. But at that moment both Witches turned upside down and were walking upon their hands. And they were so astonished, their eyes nearly popped out.

"Dear me, something has happened!" cried Wanda Witch. "How can we catch the Raggedys when we are standing on our heads and walking on our hands?"

And the Raggedys and little Ned Gnome ran around the two Witches crying, "Here we are. Why don't you catch us?"

The two Witches jumped as well as they could on their hands, but they went this way and that way, and, of course, could not catch the Raggedys at all. When the Raggedys and little Ned Gnome had grown tired of teasing the Witches, they decided to leave them. Raggedy Ann cried, "When we get three miles from here, you will be able to stand on your feet again."

And the Witches had to walk around on their hands for half an hour, because the Raggedys and little Ned Gnome took their time as they walked through the deep, deep woods. Then, when the two old witches finally were able to stand upon

their feet again, they were so tired they had to sit down.

"Just you wait, Winda!" Wanda Witch said as she wiped her red face with a red hanky. "When we catch the Raggedys, we will soon have the Wishing Pebble and the Wishing Stick. That will make up for all the trouble the Raggedys have caused us."

Of course, the two mean old Witches, just as some other people do, thought that it was the Raggedys' fault when they got into trouble. But really when a person is always getting into trouble, it's most always because he has tried to do things he should not have done. And so, each time the two witches got into trouble, it was because they wished to do something wrong.

So the two mean Witches were very unhappy and very angry as they sat and rested. The more they rested, the more unhappy and angry they became. Finally, jumping to her feet, Wanda Witch said, "Now we will chase the Raggedys!" and she picked up the flying broom.

Wanda and Winda Witch both climbed upon the magic broom and were soon flying through the woods after the Raggedys.

When the Raggedys left the two mean little old Witches walking on their hands, they could not decide what to do. Little Ned Gnome wanted to go back and visit Grampy Groundhog, but Raggedy Ann suggested that it would be nice to walk through the deep, deep woods and see some of their woodland friends. Then Raggedy Andy had an idea. "We have not seen our friend Betsy Bonnet String for a long time. We will have to go through the deep, deep woods to get to her house. So if we set out to visit her, we can see the woodland folk too."

Little Ned Gnome liked this idea, and they all thought it would be great fun. So through the deep, deep woods they walked and ran and scampered. Soon they came to a jolly group of woodland folk who were playing games together. While they played, they drank delicious sodas from the magic soda-water fountain near by.

"Hello, Hennie Hedgehog and Henrietta Hedgehog and Evelyn Elk and Eddie Elk and everybody!" the Raggedys cried and then they introduced little Ned Gnome to all their friends.

"Have you seen Betsy Bonnet String lately?" Raggedy Ann asked Eddie Elk.

"No, I haven't, Raggedy Ann!" Eddie Elk replied. "She has been away for a long time helping the meadow folk. But I expect she is home by this time. Why don't you pay her a visit? You know," he explained to little Ned Gnome, "Betsy Bonnet String can work the best magic you ever saw and she is always making fine magical things for the woodland folk—soda-water trees

71

and lollypop fields and ice-cream mud puddles and everything."

"She must be a very kindly person," little Ned Gnome said.

"Indeed she is!" Eddie Elk said. "But who in the world are these two scowling persons coming through the woods on a flying broom?"

"Oh dear!" Raggedy Ann said. "Those are two mean little old Witches who are chasing Raggedy Andy and me, trying to get our Wishing Pebble and Wishing Stick!" But when the two mean little old Witches jumped from the flying broom and ran toward the Raggedys, all the little woodland folk threw their glasses of soda at them.

"Wowie, oh wow!" the two Witches howled as they hopped upon the flying broom and flew away. "We will catch Raggedy Ann and Raggedy Andy after they leave you woodland folk. Just you wait!" they howled at the Raggedys. "You had better watch out, for we shall capture you and take the magical Wishing Things away from you!"

And the Raggedys, and little Ned Gnome, and all the woodland folk laughed loudly and drank many more glasses of soda.

My, you should have seen the two mean creatures though! They were not used to having icy cold water poured down their backs, and it made them shake and shiver all the way home.

But the Raggedys were having a good time drinking sodas and playing games with their woodland friends until it was time for them to be going to visit Betsy Bonnet String.

CHAPTER 7

The two little old Witches had finally come to
Wanda Witch's house and were changing into
clean dresses. Suddenly Winda Witch exclaimed,
"Wanda Witch, we must think of another way
to catch the Raggedys so they cannot get us into
trouble again. I know. We will get out our
magical charms and work some magic so that
the Raggedys will get lost."

"Good!" said Wanda Witch and quickly got
out all her magic charms and put them in a circle
on the floor. Then Winda put all of her magic
charms next to Wanda's. The two Witches made
quite a sight as they hopped around, saying the
magic words and making their selfish wishes.

When Raggedy Ann and Raggedy Andy and
little Ned Gnome left their woodland friends in
the deep, deep woods, they quickly decided to find

their friend Betsy Bonnet String's house. Betsy Bonnet String was a very kind-hearted person who could work the most wonderful magic. She had helped the Raggedys many times. Raggedy Ann and Raggedy Andy hoped she would help them escape from the two mean Witches.

"I cannot seem to remember which way to go," Raggedy Ann said suddenly.

"Then if we do not know which way to go, we must be lost!" Raggedy Andy exclaimed.

"Oh, no, Raggedy Andy, because even if we cannot find Betsy Bonnet String's house, we will just walk along until we come to some other place. And even if we are lost, it doesn't matter because we are in search of adventures anyhow."

Of course, the Raggedys and little Ned Gnome did not know it, but the two little old mean Witches were right behind them, snooping along and listening to the Raggedys talking.

"They do not know which way to go," Wanda Witch whispered to Winda. "Our magic charms worked fine!" Wanda whispered back. "They will just walk along and before they know it, they will walk right into my little house! Then we will capture them and take the Wishing Pebble and the Wishing Stick away from the Raggedys."

And so the three friends found themselves walking along in some very strange woods. But they were not afraid at all because they did not

know that the two little Witches had charmed them into walking right into Wanda Witch's house!

Suddenly the Raggedys and little Ned Gnome stopped, for to their surprise they found themselves inside a little house.

"Why," little Ned Gnome cried, "where are we?"

"I do not know," Raggedy Andy said unhappily. "I think this is Wanda Witch's house."

"Aha!" Wanda and Winda laughed. "You are right, Raggedy Andy. This time we have you and we shall soon have the Magic Wishing Pebble and Wishing Stick."

"That is stealing," said Raggedy Ann, "for the magic Wishing Things belong to Raggedy Andy and me. And stealing is wrong."

"Ha, ha, ha!" Wanda and Winda laughed, as they picked up a pair of scissors and got ready to snip open the Raggedys' cotton-stuffed bodies. "We do not care. We will soon have the Wishing

Stick!" and with that Wanda Witch snipped nine stitches out of Raggedy Andy's shirt and pulled the magical Wishing Stick out of the nice clean, white cotton stuffing. Raggedy Andy just kept on smiling even though Wanda Witch had taken the scissors and snipped open his cotton-stuffed body and had taken the magical Wishing Stick from its hiding place.

"You mean little old Witch!" cried Raggedy Ann. "That Wishing Stick belongs to Raggedy Andy, and it is not right for you to take it. You'll be sorry!"

"No we won't, Raggedy Ann!" Wanda Witch laughed.

"Let's make a wish right away with the magic Wishing Stick," Winda Witch said to her cousin.

"All right," Wanda Witch said. "What shall we wish for?"

"Let's both wish for new dresses," Wanda Witch said as she held the magic Wishing Stick

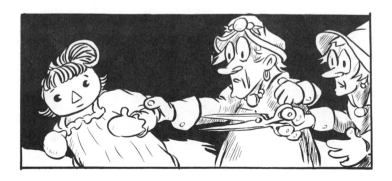

in her hand. "Let us wish for nice, shiny, new, rustly silk dresses."

The Witches held their breath and waited, but the new dresses did not appear. Nothing happened. The Witches waited another minute, but still nothing happened.

"Ha!" Wanda Witch said. "Something is wrong."

"Of course it is," Ned Gnome said. "It was wrong to take Raggedy Andy's magic Wishing Stick. That's the trouble!"

"No sir!" screamed Wanda Witch. "It is because we haven't got Raggedy Ann's magical Wishing Pebble. We must snip the Wishing Pebble out of Raggedy Ann's cotton-stuffed body!"

"It won't work a bit better than my Wishing Stick did!" Raggedy Andy laughed.

"Keep still, Raggedy Andy," howled Wanda Witch. And then because she was so angry, she screamed, "I know how to fix you. I shall put you

into a cigar box so that you will stay quiet." And into the cigar box she pushed Raggedy Andy, folding his rag arms and legs over his face so that he could fit inside. Then she shut the lid and put the cigar box in the closet.

"Now we will snip open Raggedy Ann's cotton-stuffed body and get the magical Wishing Pebble!" Winda Witch laughed.

"Ah!" Wanda Witch cried as she poked her finger around in Raggedy Ann's cotton stuffing. "Here it is! Isn't it pretty?" And she held up the magical Wishing Pebble, bright and shiny.

"Now we can make our wishes come true! Let's wish again for new dresses, Winda Witch!" So the two Witches wished again for nice, shiny, new, rustly silk dresses.

But nothing happened.

"Aha!" Little Ned Gnome laughed when the dresses did not appear and he saw the look on the Witches' faces. "The Wishing Stick and the Wishing Pebble do not work for you!"

"We will put Raggedy Ann and little Ned Gnome in the closet until they show us how to work magic with the magic Wishing Things!" Wanda Witch howled. And into the closet the mean Witches stuffed Raggedy Ann and little Ned Gnome.

Now all three friends were in the closet. Raggedy Andy was stuffed in the cigar box, his arms and legs folded over his face, but that did not keep him from smiling just as he always did. But little Ned Gnome was not smiling and he whispered to Raggedy Ann who still had a smile on her face, "How will we ever escape?"

"Maybe we shall and maybe not, little Ned Gnome," Raggedy Ann replied. "But one thing

I know for sure is that the two mean little Witches will never be able to make their wishes come true with the magical Wishing Stick and the magical Wishing Pebble, because just before they took the Wishing Pebble from me I wished that none of their wishes would come true!"

"Maybe something will happen and we will be able to escape from the two mean little Witches," little Ned Gnome said hopefully.

But the two mean Witches had heard him and through the keyhole they howled, "Oh, no, little Ned Gnome, you shall never, never escape, now that we have you stuffed in the closet!"

Then Wanda Witch said to Winda, "One thing is sure, Winda Witch, we do not seem able to make our wishes come true with these things, so let us get out our charms and find out just why this is happening to us."

So the two mean little Witches got out all their charms and danced about them and in two minutes they knew that Raggedy Ann had made a wish for the magical Wishing Things not to work for the Witches.

This made the Witches very, very angry.

"Now we will take Raggedy Ann from the closet," said Wanda Witch, "and run her through the clothes wringer! That will make her wish again with the Wishing Pebble for our wishes to come true!"

Wanda Witch unlocked the closet door and

called, "Raggedy Ann, you must come out and make a wish for our wishes to come true when we use the Wishing Pebble and Wishing Stick!"

But Raggedy Ann did not answer the mean Witch.

"Hurry up, Raggedy Ann!" Wanda Witch howled. "If you do not come out right away, I shall pull you out!" When Raggedy Ann still did not answer, Wanda Witch swung the door wide open and reached inside. She meant to catch Raggedy Ann by her rag head and pull her out, but instead she gave a startled scream, for the closet was empty!

Raggedy Ann and little Ned Gnome had completely disappeared.

"How could they have got out of the closet when we have been right here in the room all the time?" Wanda Witch yelled.

"Perhaps someone put us to sleep, and while we were asleep, the person unlocked the closet door and let Raggedy Ann and little Ned Gnome escape!" Winda Witch answered.

Raggedy Andy, who had been squeezed into a cigar box and then put in the closet, heard what the two little old mean Witches said, and he was so glad to hear that his friends had escaped that he yelled as loudly as he could, "Ha, ha, ha, I'm glad! Goody! Goody!"

You can just imagine how angry this made Wanda and Winda Witch.

Wanda Witch picked up the little cigar box and shook it very hard. "There," she cried, "if you do not keep still, I will shake you until your teeth rattle!"

"Ha, ha, ha!" Raggedy Andy laughed as hard

as he had before! "I haven't any teeth! My mouth is just painted on! Ha, ha, ha!"

This was more than Wanda Witch could stand, so she opened the cigar box and reached in to drag Raggedy Andy out and shake him, even if he didn't have any teeth!

With a loud scream, "He's gone too!" she dropped the cigar box and sat down hard on the floor!

"Someone is playing a joke on us, Wanda Witch!" Winda cried. "Where could Raggedy Andy have gone so quickly? He was in the box when you held it in your hand! I heard him; didn't you?"

"Indeed I did!" Wanda replied weakly. Then she brightened a bit and said, "Well, it saves us the trouble of running them through the clothes wringer. Pick up the little cigar box, Winda, and put it up on the mantelpiece."

Winda stooped to pick up the cigar box, but just as she reached down, the box flew up in the air and went *"Bop"* right on her nose, then fell with a crash on the floor again.

"Wow!" Winda Witch screamed. "If you want the cigar box put upon the mantelpiece, you will have to put it there yourself!"

"You are a lazy Witch," Wanda cried and stooped over to pick it up herself. But she too was hit by the cigar box with a *"Bop"* on her nose.

Then both little Witches howled and ran out the door yelling, "Let's get out of here!"

As soon as they were out the door, the sound of merry laughter could be heard, and, of course, it was Raggedy Ann and Raggedy Andy and little Ned Gnome, laughing until their sides ached.

Finally Raggedy Ann said, "What happened?"

"I do not know!" Raggedy Andy replied, "I was in the cigar box all the time until it dropped on the floor and then I rolled out!"

"And we were in the closet until the Witches opened the door. Then we walked out!" little Ned Gnome said. "Can you see me, Raggedy Ann and Raggedy Andy?"

"No! Where are you?" Raggedy Ann and Raggedy Andy said.

"I'm right here," said little Ned Gnome, "but I can't see you either!"

"Now we *are* in a pickle!" Raggedy Andy said to Raggedy Ann and little Ned Gnome. "Here we are, captured by the two mean little old Witches and our magical Wishing Pebble and Wishing Stick taken from us. And we are invisible!"

"Maybe they left the magic Wishing Things here in the house," Raggedy Ann suggested. "And since they belong to us, it is only right that we should take them, if we can find them. Let's all search together!"

So the three friends searched in all the little

rooms, in the closets, and everywhere. But it was no use; they could not find the magic Wishing Things.

"The Witches must have them in their pockets," Raggedy Ann sighed. "If we only could find them, we could wish ourselves miles away from here!"

"Now I will tell you what I think we must do," little Ned Gnome said. "I think the Witches will be coming back here soon, and when they do, they must not know that we are here. Then, we will try to get the magic Wishing Things away from them and wish ourselves far away from here."

"That is a very good idea, little Ned Gnome—" Raggedy Ann laughed—"but we must keep very still, and we must watch that they do not step on us!"

Very soon, little Ned Gnome heard the Witches coming and he warned his friends to be quiet. The little old Witches came into the house and sat down in their rocking chairs.

"What do you think could have happened?" Wanda asked Winda.

"I do not know," Winda answered. "But anyway, we have the Wishing Stick and the Wishing Pebble!"

"But our wishes do not come true," Wanda Witch said, "so the Wishing Pebble and Wishing Stick do us no good!"

"We must get on our magic flying broom and find the Raggedys and make them tell us how to get the magic Wishing Things to work for us!"

So they quickly hopped on the flying broom and sailed right out the front door. Although the Witches did not know it, sitting in back of them were Raggedy Ann, Raggedy Andy and little Ned Gnome. As they went flying through the woods, Winda said, "The flying broom is acting very strange, Wanda! Here we are flying through the woods and the flying broom acts as though it does not know where to go!"

"This is the first time the flying broom has ever failed to find the Raggedys," Wanda Witch said.

Of course, because it could not talk, the flying broom could not tell them that the Raggedys and little Ned Gnome were sitting right behind them. So the broom just flew around in a circle.

Finally Wanda Witch said, "I believe something has taken the magic out of the flying broom

or it would take us to where the Raggedys are! Let's stop and get our magic charms and see what the trouble is!"

When the Witches hopped off their magic flying broom, the Raggedys and little Ned Gnome hopped off right behind them. But the Witches could not see them because they were invisible.

The two witches got out all their charms and then put the Magical Wishing Stick and the Wishing Pebble alongside.

"Maybe if we put the magical Wishing Things in the center of our magic ring with the other charms, the Wishing Stick and Wishing Pebble will make our wishes come true!" Wanda Witch said.

Inside the magic ring which they drew on the ground were a bent safety pin, a piece of blue glass from a broken bottle, a grasshopper's left leg, two horse hairs, a red bean and a shingle nail. They were all very magical.

"Higgledy piggledy, my black hen!" Wanda

Witch sang as she and her cousin danced about the magic circle.

Then a strange, queer thing happened! The magical Wishing Pebble rolled around inside the circle until it came to the tip of the magical Wishing Stick. Then the Wishing Stick stood right up with the Wishing Pebble balanced on its end. As the two Witches held their breath, the Wishing Stick and the Wishing Pebble flew straight through the air. As they flew away, the Witches heard the laughter of three people: Raggedy Ann, Raggedy Andy, and little Ned Gnome.

"Oh dear," cried the two Witches, "the Raggedys and little Ned Gnome have fooled us again!" And they were crying so hard they forgot to run after the magical Wishing Things. And this was how the Raggedys and little Ned Gnome escaped.

As the three friends ran through the deep, deep woods, laughing, Raggedy Ann asked, "What I would like to know, Ned Gnome, is whether you took the magical Wishing Things, or did Raggedy Andy?"

Little Ned Gnome answered, "I guess it was Raggedy Andy, for I did not."

"Oh, no! Raggedy Andy said, "I did not pick up the magical Wishing Things! Didn't you take them, Raggedy Ann?"

"No!" Raggedy Ann said. "Oh, dear, now we

are invisible and our Wishing Things have disappeared too! What shall we do?"

"I don't know," little Ned Gnome answered. "But I would like to find out who made us invisible."

Then, while the Raggedys stood there, wondering who it could have been, they heard someone say, "Oof, Oof!"

And Raggedy Ann knew right away, "It's Percival Pig! It must have been he who made us invisible, and he has made himself invisible, too. He must have taken our magical Wishing Things!"

"Then we shall never get them back again," Raggedy Andy said sadly. "For Percival Pig helped the Witches capture us once before!"

Then the Raggedys and little Ned Gnome were surprised to hear Percival Pig laugh, "Ha, ha, ha! This time I have really fooled you. It was I who made you invisible and helped you escape from the two Witches and it was I who took the magical Wishing Things for you! See, here they are!"

All at once, the Raggedys and little Ned Gnome could see the magical Wishing Stick and the Wishing Pebble.

"Now, I shall make you visible," Percival Pig said. And suddenly the Raggedys and little Ned Gnome could all see one another again. But they

could not see Percival Pig, even though they could hear him say, "Take the Wishing Things, for they are yours!"

CHAPTER 8

"Thank you, thank you, Percival Pig!" Raggedy Ann and Raggedy Andy said together. And Raggedy Ann went on to ask him, "Now will you tell us why you helped us escape from the Witches, when once before you helped Wanda Witch capture us? And why have you given the magical Wishing Things back to us when once you wanted them for yourself?"

"Yes, I will tell you why I did those things," Percival Pig said. "But I think I had better tell you my whole story right from the beginning."

The Raggedys could not see Percival Pig but they could hear him sigh as he said this.

"It must be a sad story," the Raggedys and Ned Gnome thought. And indeed it proved to be. Raggedy Ann, Raggedy Andy and Ned Gnome sat and listened to the story as Percival Pig told it.

"A long, long time ago, when I was a little boy," he said, "I wanted everything I saw. When I went anywhere with my mother or father, I always teased for this and for that. And if they did not buy me everything I asked for, I would get very whiny and I would stamp my feet and say, 'Oh beans, why can't I have it?' And I grew worse and worse until one day when I went through the woods alone, I saw a funny little old woman who asked, 'Percival, would you like to have a nice ring with a red ruby in it—one that will make all your wishes come true?' Of course I said I would, and the old woman gave it to me and then she laughed and laughed. I did not know then why she laughed, but afterward I found out."

And then Percival Pig had to stop to dry his eyes, for he had been crying as he told them his sad story.

"Well, to go on with my tale: As soon as I put the ring on my finger, I made a wish and I even forgot to thank the old woman, I was so busy wishing. Oh, I wished for this and I wished for that, until I wished for everything I could think of! Still I wasn't satisfied and I wished that I had something else to wish for! I made a pig of myself wishing for this and that. And the first thing

I knew, I had truly changed right into a little
squealy pig!"

Here Percival Pig stopped and cried as though
his heart would break. He sobbed, "Then my
sister, Penelope, met the little old woman, and
she took a wishing ring that the old woman gave
her, and soon she too was a pig like me!"

"And are you still a pig now?" Raggedy Ann
asked, smiling.

"No!" Percival Pig replied. "The other day
the funny old woman came to me and said, 'If
you want to change from a pig to a real boy
again, I will give you the wishing ring! But it
will work only if you wish for things to make

others happy. And if you use it to make others happy, you will be a real boy again!' So I took it and I wished to help you. So now I am a boy again, but I am still invisible!"

As they all sat thinking about this story, Percival added, "I have tried to become visible

again, but I don't seem able to make the wish come true—maybe because it is not a wish to make someone else happy!"

"Hmmm," Raggedy Ann thought. "Let me try wishing it for you with the magical Wishing Pebble!"

And as Raggedy Ann made her wish, right there before them, in plain sight, stood Percival, a smiling, happy little boy.

After Percival had thanked the Raggedys, he asked, "Will you help me find my sister Penelope? She is still a pig, but I know she would like to be a little girl again."

So through the woods they all went and soon they found Penelope Pig and when she had been changed into a smiling, gay little girl again, the three friends and Percival and Penelope romped along till they came upon the ice-cream-soda fountain.

"Just what I needed after this adventure," said Raggedy Ann, and she made ice-cream sodas

for all her friends and for herself, too, of course.

As they finished their sodas, who should come flying up but the two little old mean Witches, Wanda and Winda!

"Oh dear," Raggedy Ann said when she saw them, "now they will try to capture us again!"

"Let's run as fast as we can!" Raggedy Andy said.

"Do not run, Raggedy Ann and Raggedy Andy," Wanda and Winda Witch cried. "We will not chase you any more!"

So the Raggedys and little Ned Gnome did not move, and the two Witches came and sat beside them on the ground.

"We shall not try to take the magical Wishing Things away from you ever again!" Wanda Witch said.

"When we had the Wishing Pebble and the Wishing Stick, we could not get them to make our wishes come true!" Winda Witch said.

"And so we have come to ask you to forgive us for causing you so much trouble, Raggedy Ann and Raggedy Andy and little Ned Gnome," Wanda Witch said.

By this time both little Witches were crying as if their hearts would break. Raggedy Ann took her pretty blue hanky and wiped the Witches' eyes and said, "Don't cry any more, Miss Wanda and Miss Winda Witch!"

Turning to Raggedy Ann and little Ned

Gnome, she asked, "We forgive them, don't we?" And Raggedy Andy and little Ned Gnome agreed with kindly little Raggedy Ann. So the two little Witches dried their tears and smiled. It was the first time that the Raggedys had seen them smile.

"Who is the pretty little girl and this nice-looking little boy with you, Raggedy Ann?" asked Wanda Witch as she looked closely at Penelope and Percival.

"They are Penelope and Percival," Raggedy Ann laughed. "They used to be Percival and Penelope Pig!"

"However did they change into a girl and boy?" asked Winda Witch in surprise.

"Why, I changed them with my magic Wishing Pebble," answered Raggedy Ann. "You see, they used to be just as they are now, before they made pigs of themselves. It was Percival who made us invisible in your house and it was Percival who helped us escape from you!"

Wanda and Winda were silent awhile as they thought this over. Then, sighing loudly, Winda Witch said, "Dear me! How often Wanda and I have wished that we were not witches. Our magic charms would not change us back into what we were before we became Witches, and many times we have cried and cried about it."

Then Percival said, "Now that I am a boy again and still have the wishing ring, I will make

the wish that you two little Witches change back into what you used to be!" And before the two little old Witches had time to blink their eyes, they had been changed into pretty young ladies —two of the prettiest young ladies the Raggedys had ever seen!

They were so happy that they hugged Percival and Penelope and Raggedy Ann and Raggedy Andy and little Ned Gnome fifteen times each. Then, after all that excitement, they all had to have some ice-cream sodas.

"I am so glad we are not mean little old Witches any more!" Winda laughed happily, and Wanda said, "Oh, I am, too!"

"And I am glad that I am not a pig any

longer," Percival and Penelope both said. "It isn't any fun being a pig!"

"Now that we are all happy again," Wanda said, "I think we must do something to sew up Raggedy Ann and Raggedy Andy where we snipped their stitches."

"Oh, that is easy," Raggedy Ann said, "I will wish for some thread and needles, and then you and Winda may sew up our seams."

After Raggedy Ann had made her wish, the two cousins placed the magical Wishing Pebble back in Raggedy Ann and the magical Wishing Stick back in Raggedy Andy and then gently

sewed up their snipped seams. And the rag dolls were just as good as new.

When they had finished, Winda and Wanda decided to try their magical charms, but although they said all the magical words they knew, they could not make a single magical thing, no matter how hard they tried.

"Well." Wanda laughed. "It is just as well, for we do not want to make magical things any more. We will just try to be kind and thoughtful to everyone, and that will be far better than being able to work magic!"

The two pretty young ladies threw their magic

charms into the bushes and turned to the Raggedys, and little Ned Gnome, and Percival and Penelope, and said, "Now we must say good-by for awhile. We must go to our little house and, after we have tidied it and made it pretty and

clean, we will be able to invite you to a party. Good-by. We will see you all very soon."

So off they went, happy indeed again to be such nice young ladies instead of two mean little old Witches. And Raggedy Ann and Raggedy Andy and their friends tripped merrily off into the deep, deep woods in search of more adventures.

THE
GRUELLE IDEAL

*It is the Gruelle ideal
that books for children
should contain nothing to
cause fright, suggest fear, glo-
rify mischief, excuse malice
or condone cruelty. That
is why they are called*
"BOOKS GOOD FOR
CHILDREN."